JACOB

ME AND MY HUMAN

LITTLE CAT TALES

BY SVEN HARTMANN

AND THOMAS HÄRTNER

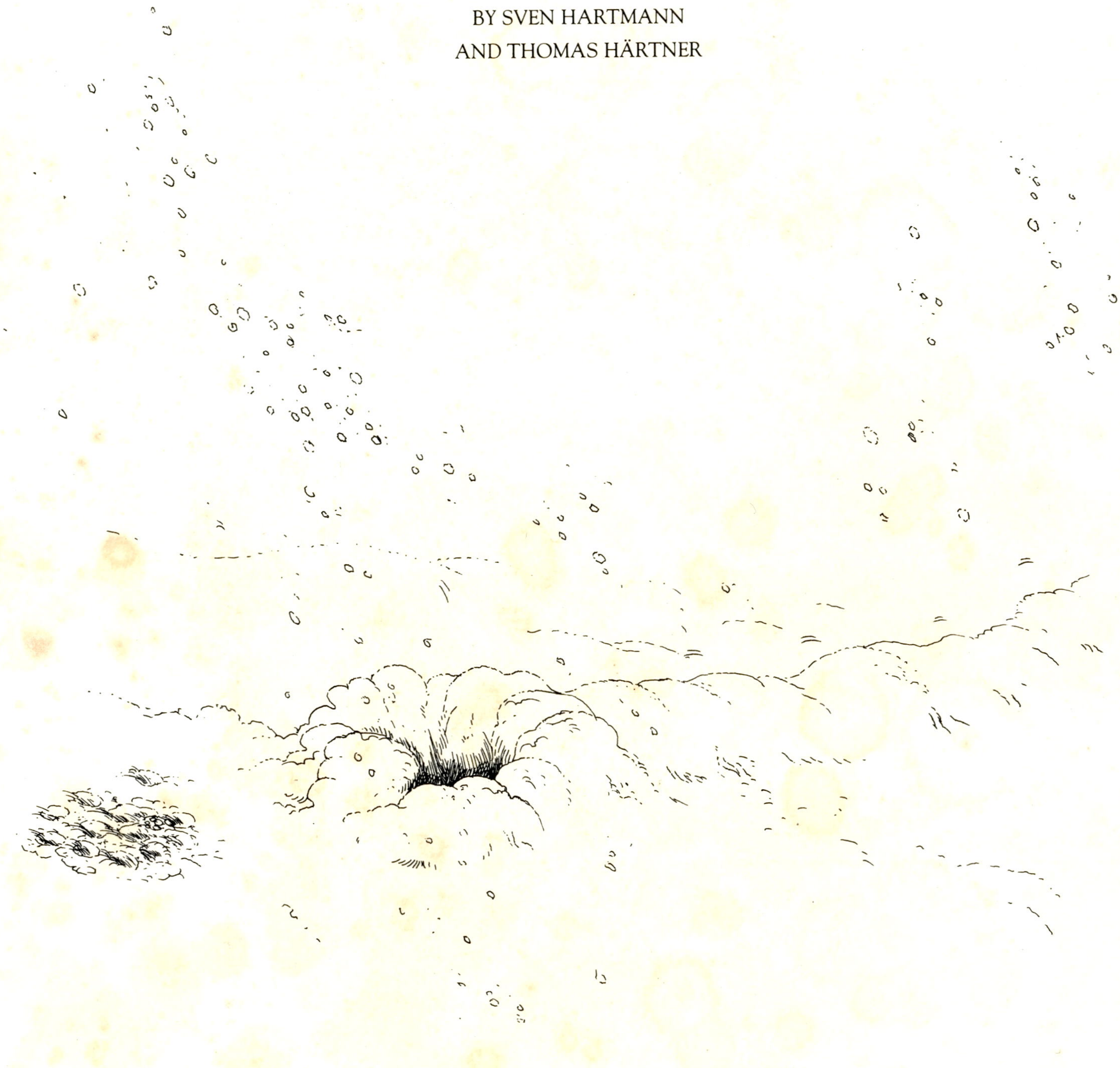

ME AND MY HUMAN
LITTLE CAT TALES

BY SVEN HARTMANN
AND THOMAS HÄRTNER

JACOB

EDITED BY JACK BERNARD
TRANSLATED BY ANGELIKA MACRI
London
BARRON'S
Woodbury, New York

PRINTED IN HONG KONG

A NEW YEAR BEGINS, or THE WISER ONE GIVES IN

I have this Human. I'm not sure that having a Human is worth the trouble, but I don't have any choice at this point. He was so nice to me when I was little that I sort of *had* to adopt him. And, of course, he jumped at the chance.

NOW I have second thoughts about the whole thing. But I guess it's too late. Besides, we do get along pretty well; and I like it a lot when he pets me and scratches my tummy. ONE problem is that we don't agree about a lot of things. Also, he has some bad habits. I guess I can handle him, but it's really hard work — especially since humans don't learn all that fast. It gets on my nerves when he wants to have his own way all the time. But, as I explained last year, I pretty much know how to handle that too.

WE'VE been living together for a year now. I don't actually know what a "year" is, but that's what my Human calls it. I think it has something to do with eating. When I've emptied more bowls of food than I can remember, that's a year — I think. Whatever it is, it's a long, long time.

Speaking of food, I must say that mine has been a real problem lately. My Human just opens this round thing with some kind of tool and empties a pile of glop into my bowl. It doesn't even smell good. He says it's "healthy," but I don't know what that means — and I don't care. I just let the stuff sit there all day.

Let me tell you how stubborn a human can be. Even though I won't eat the glop, he refuses to give me anything else! Sometimes I try to show him what I think of this food by scratching the floor around the bowl — just the way I do inside my box. But he doesn't catch on.

Sometimes, when he's not there, I do eat a *little* of it — just around the edges, so he can't tell.

In the old days, I used to get pieces of meat and liver, all cut up and so tender that I hardly had to chew. I get hungry just thinking about it. But the stuff I get now is hardly worth eating!

MAYBE my Human has lost his mind. He never leaves the apartment anymore — he just lies around in our bed all day, making snorting sounds with that great big nose of his. Believe me, it's scary. Then he rubs his nose with a piece of cloth. And he keeps making these funny noises with his chest.

EVEN worse, he hardly ever talks to me or pets me anymore. And he keeps shivering, even though it's no longer cold and there's no more of that fluffy white stuff outside the window. He's been drinking a lot of steaming hot yellow water that makes drops of water suddenly appear on his forehead. It also makes him giggle and talk to himself. I can tell by the things he says that he's not talking to *me*. I think maybe it's all some kind of trick to make me eat that awful glop in my bowl. I guess I'll have to give in so he'll stop acting so strange.

SPRING, or THE BLACK THING

MY Human is feeling better now, but he still isn't entirely normal.

TRUE, he doesn't just lie in bed anymore,
and he's stopped making those horrible noises with his nose and chest.
But he still doesn't pay much attention to me.
He spends a lot of time staring out the window; when I sit on the sill next to him, he just ignores me.
And he doesn't laugh anymore. And that really bugs me.

IT might be those little fuzzy balls outside the window that go "peep! peep!" all day.
Maybe what's wrong with my Human is that he'd like to catch one of them
but doesn't know how. There are lots of them now that it's nice and warm outside.
THEY'RE always flying around and hopping from limb to limb. I know how my Human feels.
When I watch the fuzzy balls flying around, I get this strange, nervous feeling inside me —
like more than anything else in the world I want to play with them, or something.

THERE are little green dots on the trees now, too, but they don't move around.
ANYWAY, I can't reach the fuzzy balls. There's something hard in the window
that blocks my way, even though I can see through it. Hard *air*, I guess.
But those fuzzy balls sure make me nervous.

MAYBE "nervous" isn't the right word to describe my feeling.
It's more like an itch deep down inside, where I can't scratch.

SOMETIMES, when I just can't stand it anymore, I run through the house as fast as I can. Or I try to catch my tail. Or I just pretend that one of the fuzzy balls is in the house with me and I have to catch it right away. But no matter what I do, the itch inside won't go away.

IT used to be that, when I did all those things, my Human would laugh and say,
"Jacob, I think you're going crazy!" — or something nice like that.

BUT now he doesn't laugh, and he doesn't say anything. What does he do? He just ignores me.

THERE is something that does make him talk and laugh, though. It's a shiny black thing that makes a funny sound (a terrible noise if you ask me). When it makes the noise, my Human runs over to it. Then he picks up half of it and presses it against his head and starts talking. His voice is all sweet then, and he turns red — especially around the ears.

HE talks to the black thing a long time, and he laughs, too. In fact, he laughs a lot more than he should, and it doesn't sound natural.

I can tell when he's about to stop talking. First his voice gets low and serious, and then he makes this disgusting wet sound with his mouth, like a smacking noise. After that, he puts the black thing back on top of the other half.

HE always goes crazy right after talking to the black thing. He hops around the room and waves his hands and says all kinds of things to me that I don't understand. Naturally, I ignore him and go sit under a chair until he's gotten over it.

I just can't stand that black thing!

EASTER, or IT'S FUN TO GO HUNTING

IT'S even warmer outside now, and everything is hopping and flying and crawling out there. I can see it all through the window. More than anything I'd like to go outside and play with all that hopping, flying, and crawling stuff. I tell my Human, but he doesn't let me. By the way, my Human has been more like his old self lately. He cares about me again. The only thing is, when he picks me up and pets me, he keeps saying this other name — and it's not "Jacob" either!

WHEN he does that, I let him know I don't like it. I sit in my box and pretend that I have to "go."

I know who that other name belongs to. There's another human who has been coming to visit us a lot. This new one has really long hair and smells different from my Human.

THE new human and mine put their heads together
and stay like that a long time. Sometimes they make strange noises, too.
It's all so dumb that I keep walking between their legs until they start laughing.

THEN the human with the long hair picks me up and says things like:
"Oh, Jacob! What a character you are!" Maybe I *am* a character,
but I still don't like the idea of getting picked up by just any human who comes along.

THE new human talks and laughs in a high, squeaky voice. I don't like it.
And I can't understand what my Human sees in the long-haired one.

21
22
23
24
25

All things considered, though, my Human understands me better than he used to. For a long time he got to do all the hunting and searching; I had to hide all the stuff for him to find. Sometimes I guess I was too good at it, because he'd get red in the face and yell things that I pretended not to understand. But even when he yelled a lot, he was always so happy when he found the stuff. Now, he's finally learned that I like to go hunting and searching too!

The other day he locked me in the room where I always eat. I could hear him rumbling around in the room where we do our playing and working. Then, after a little while, he left the house — but not before he opened the door of my room just a bit, so I could push through. Well, believe it or not, my Human had hidden things for me in the other room! He really is learning fast.

I was pretty excited, so it didn't take me long to start finding what he had hid. Under our bed, behind the curtains — pretty much everywhere — there were these hard, colored balls sitting in curly green stuff. I even found some in the basket where he throws the paper when he thinks I don't look good on it. (That's how we work. I sit there, and he makes lines on paper until the lines look like me, more or less).

THESE hard balls are really nice. They roll around just right — never in a straight line, so that you can always be surprised. When they hit against something, they make a wonderful cracking noise and the color chips off. Then you can see the white inside, and it doesn't smell bad. In fact, it doesn't taste bad, either, and pretty soon I wasn't hungry anymore.

THE curly green stuff was really nice, too. It crinkled and rustled,
and I played with it a lot and finally put it in our bed.
I thought that maybe my Human and I would play with it some more later.
While I was stuffing some of it under his pillow, I found a little box with pretty paper around it.
It was a lot of work getting it open, but I didn't mind
because I thought my Human had put something nice inside for me.

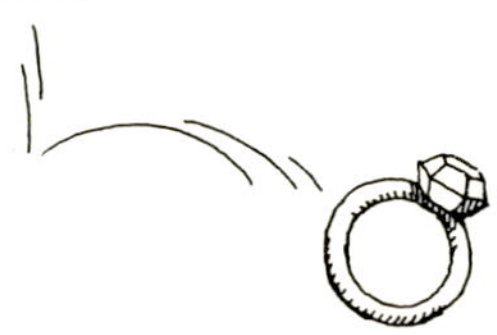

I don't know what it was.
It didn't have any smell and it was round and narrow and hard, and you could see through it.
What a disappointment!
So I threw it away, and it rolled under the grill by the window
(where it always stays all nice and warm, even when it's cold outside).

By then I wasn't feeling all that happy anymore, so I waited for my Human by the door.
I kept calling him — just so that when he did come, he'd know that I was glad to see him.
Unfortunately, he showed up with that long-haired human.
But when he saw what a good job I had done in finding all the stuff he had hidden for me,
he was so happy that he let out a loud moan. Then he yelled, "Where's thc ring?"
and started looking all over the room. Obviously, he wanted to play hide-and-seek too.
I was really glad about that, and I tried to help him.
After all, I knew where everything was.

But he wanted to search all by himself and he pushed me aside. Humans are selfish that way.
He was really puffing and panting by the time he found the round, hard thing.
Also, he made that happy moaning sound again.
I was proud of him for finding the thing and tried to show him how I felt. But he just muttered
"Oh Jacob, Jacob!" in a peculiar tone of voice. I'm not sure what he meant by that.

THE SUMMER BEGINS, or THE DOG

So many things have been happening around here that I have a lot to think about.
To start with, I'm not even sure that I should ever speak to my Human again.
It all started one day when I was alone and having a really good time
playing with these black dots that are always flying around in our apartment.
After awhile I lay down in the nice, warm light that comes from far away through our window,
and I started thinking about playing with those fuzzy balls that go "peep."
I could see them hopping and flying around the trees.
They can hide really well now,
since the green dots on the trees have grown so big. And the big dots flap around so much now
that sometimes I can't tell if it's really a dot or one of the fuzzy balls.

I had an idea, so I sat still and listened for my Human to come home. (I can tell it's him long before he opens the door, because of his footsteps.) Then, when he finally got home and opened the door, I jumped over his big black paws and just kept on going — out the door and down some thick boards till I reached the ground. I had never done that before; and, wow, was my Human yelling to beat the band!

Of course, I was scared — just a little. But I kept going till I reached this wall.
There were a lot of cracks in it, so I squeezed through one of them.

Well, I've never been so amazed in all my life!
I didn't know there were that many humans in the whole world.
And there were these big shiny boxes that roared and ran around even faster than I can.
I scrunched down and walked real low against the wall for awhile. Then I sat down and began cleaning my paws,
because I didn't want anybody to think I was new around here.

45

Before I could take a really good look around, I saw a human coming with someone who, at first glance, looked just like me. But then I saw that, although he did have black and white spots, he was bigger. Just a little bigger, of course.

Now this is the funny part: the one with the spots had his human tied at the end of a string, so that the human had to follow him around. Incredible!

When he saw me, he stopped so short that his human almost ran into him. Then he stood staring at me and moving his tail back and forth as fast as he could. I tried to do the same with my tail, but it just didn't work very well.

SUDDENLY, the one with the spots began making the strangest noises: first some real short, chopped-off grunts, and then something that sounded like purring, except louder. Then he began pulling his human toward me.

WHEN he did that, I made myself look real fat and hunched my back, and I made the same almost-purring noise he had. And it really worked! I was so impressed! He must have been impressed too, because he stopped short and said nothing at all.

THEN all of a sudden my Human appeared out of nowhere and grabbed me in his arms. The one with the spots made his chopped-off noises again, and his human said to mine: "That's the first time I've ever heard a cat growl like a dog." And my Human said, "Oh, yes. He always does that." Then he carried me back into our apartment. I felt really proud of my adventure. And it also felt good to have my Human carry me in his arms. But then he ruined the whole thing by slapping my behind with one of his front paws — *hard*!

WOW, was that unpleasant! I didn't have any idea why he was so worked up. So, I scratched him a little — just enough to let him know what I thought about the whole thing. Then I jumped out of his arms and crawled under our bed. At that point, I really gave him a piece of my mind.

I calmed down pretty quick after that and, all things considered, I was pleased with myself.
Now at least I know what a "dog" is: he makes these loud, chopped-off noises,
purrs funny, wags his tail like it's going to fall off,
and leads his human around on a string.
I would never do something like that to my Human.
I know he needs his freedom.

THE SHAKING BOX

My Human likes to have his own way, and I (being more clever) usually try to humor him. After all, he is only human — which means that he doesn't understand things the way *we* do. Still, it isn't always easy to be patient with him. Yesterday, for instance, I finally realized that my Human is simply incapable of original thinking. All he can do is imitate others.

It was still very early and we were just finishing our breakfast. I felt quite comfortable, with my tummy full and my Human petting me. Then, suddenly, he put something around my neck. There was a string tied to it — just like the string that that dog had tied to his human. No doubt, that's where my Human got the idea. Human see, human do. But he didn't have to be so sneaky about it.

Naturally, I tried my best to get the thing off me. I tried pulling it over my head with my paws, running all over the apartment, rolling over — nothing worked. And to make matters worse, I got all tangled up in the thing.

It goes without saying that my Human thought it was all very funny. Don't ask me why —
I never did understand his sense of humor.
I don't think I'll ever figure him out.
Why on earth would he want me to lead him around on a string?
So, I just lay there on the floor and glared at him.
Then he picked me up, put me on his shoulder, and said soft things to me —
which comes from having a bad conscience.

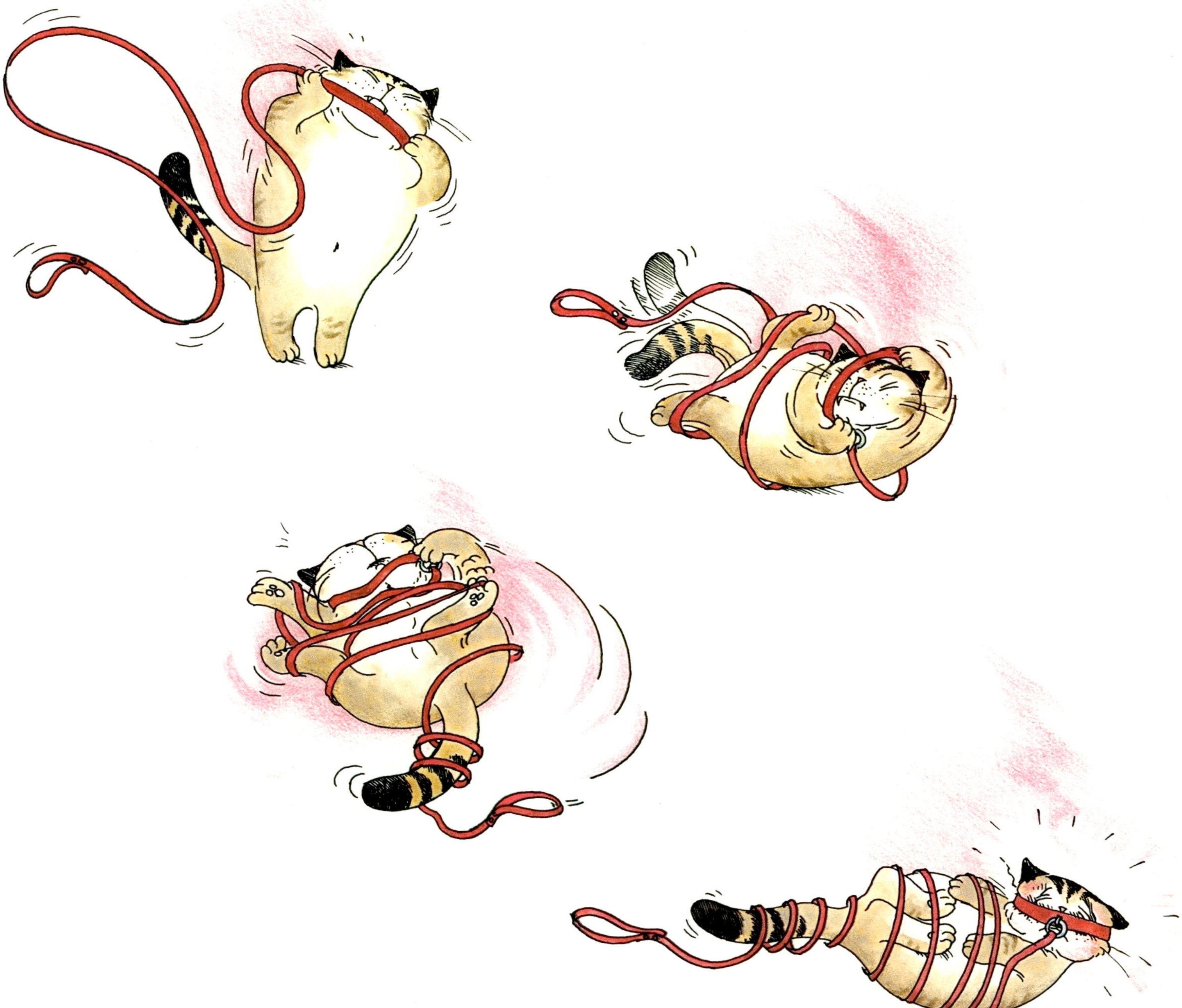

BUT then he carried me out the front door and down those boards
with the thing still around my neck. I didn't want to go outside again, because
I was still thinking about the dog and the spanking I got. But I *had* to know what was out there;
so I decided to let him have his way one more time.
OUTSIDE were all the noises and smells again, and all those humans. It made me want to go
right back inside. But my Human clutched me tight and said that I was very brave.
I am, of course; but I would rather have been inside his shirt all the same.

THEN my Human crawled into this big box with me. The other human,
the one with the long hair, was already there. But I was too mixed up to care.
SUDDENLY, the box made a horrible noise and started to shake and rattle all over.
The shaking went right through me, and I jumped off my Human and crawled into a dark corner.
But the shaking and the noise continued.

IN fact, it got worse: all at once the box jolted forward like it had gone crazy.
I tried closing my eyes, but that didn't make it stop either.
MY Human began talking softly to me again and tugged on that dumb string around my neck,
but I stayed right where I was.
I couldn't figure out why he was doing this to me, but
I had already decided that he'd pay for it one way or another. In fact, I was already thinking
about what I could do to him at home to keep him from pulling this stunt again.
I would have thought of something, too,
except that with all the shaking and the noise my stomach was turning somersaults.

Before too long, I felt all right again and decided to have a look around. I climbed over my Human — pretending that I didn't see him, naturally — and jumped to the back of the box where there was a window.

It had that hard air in it, just like our window at home. By then, I wasn't so nervous anymore, and I noticed something really strange: the trees. Our trees at home stand still and just move their green dots sometimes. But the trees outside this box were running past us so fast that I could hardly even see them!

I was thinking hard about that when my Human interrupted me to say,
"Are you all right, Jacob? It's not all that bad, is it?"
And he tried to pet me.
Of course, I didn't even look at him, much less let him touch me.
You have to be firm with humans or you lose control completely.

Still, I have to admit that, once you get used to the noise and the shaking,
the box isn't all that bad. But I'm not about to tell him that.
I'll just let him suffer for awhile.

THE PICNIC, or THE GIANT DOG

Now I'm not mad at my Human anymore about the big-box incident. After all, I did get to see a lot of interesting things that we don't have at home. I think I'd better explain what I mean.

JUST when I had gotten used to the noise and the shaking, it stopped. My Human took me out of the box and put me on the ground, which was covered with long green fur (or maybe hair; I can never keep them straight). It was nice and soft, and it tickled my nose.

WELL, if my Human thought he was going to get me to lead him around on that string, he was very much mistaken. As soon as he tried it, I threw myself flat on the ground and wouldn't budge.

Believe it or not, he actually understood what was going on and untied the string. He did leave that other thing around my neck — but I'll think of a way to get rid of that, too.

MEANWHILE, the human with the long hair had taken a basket and some blankets from the big box. Both of them sat on one of the blankets with the basket between them. I know why, too — I could smell that there was something good to eat in the basket. But when my Human tried to give me some, I just wasn't interested. All that shaking inside the big box had ruined my appetite.

BESIDES, I wanted to look around this new place.

THE green fur smelled good. I even tried chewing it. It didn't taste bad, and though it sort of pricked my mouth, I ate some of it anyway. If it wasn't real food or real fur, what was it? I gave up trying to figure it out and went a little bit farther — making sure that I could still keep an eye on my Human. HE does get me mad sometimes, but it's nice to know he's there.

THERE was a beautiful flower only a few steps away from me. It was all by itself — not like at home, where there are always a lot of flowers in one pot. This one wasn't in a pot at all, and it had a more interesting smell than those at home. I sniffed it for a long time.

WHAT really surprised me, though, were the flowers that fly. As I walked around, some of the flowers flew off other flowers and went up in the air! They fluttered around for awhile, and then came back down to the ground and turned into flowers again.

I was so surprised that I had to sit down and think about that for awhile. Later, I caught one of the flying flowers, but it didn't have any smell at all. It just fluttered.

It's too bad that I couldn't find any of those fuzzy balls that go "peep." I could hear them, but I couldn't see them.

THERE were lots of other noises, too — nice noises, and not too loud. There were yellow and black dots buzzing around the flowers. And then there were green dots, but not like the green dots on trees — these dots made shrill noises.

I couldn't see them at first, so I tried sneaking up on one of the noises. Of course, I was very quiet but the sound stopped almost as soon as I moved. Then suddenly the dot jumped away! It was very exciting, and I wanted to catch the dot in the worst way, but it was almost impossible to see it in all that green stuff. Also, the dot could jump almost as far as I could. Every time I landed where it was supposed to be, it had already jumped somewhere else. In fact, there were so many green dots jumping around, and brown ones too, that I just couldn't decide which to chase. So I sat down and pretended that I wasn't even interested in them.

I was just about ready to try again when I saw something that made me scrunch down fast. Not far away from me there was this dog — I *guess* it was a dog — with black and white spots. I shouldn't have been afraid. But this one was different. For one thing, he was much, much bigger — even bigger than my Human. Also, he had a pouch or bag of some kind that he carried from his belly. And he had four ears.

WHEN he looked at me with those gigantic eyes, I couldn't help growling a little; but when I did, the dog let out a sound like I had never heard before — loud, and deep, and long! It was horrible.

THIS dog was too much for me.
As fast as I could, I ran back to the spot where I had left my Human.

BUT there was nobody around — only the big box. So I ran over to it and hopped on top.
THEN I saw my Human and the one with the long hair.
They were lying on the green stuff, rubbing their heads together again.
They couldn't have cared less about the giant dog.
I jumped between them and nuzzled against my Human, pretending
that I just wanted to play.

I jumped around a lot,
and every time I jumped I looked to see where the dog was.
I wasn't afraid anymore, because he was pretty far away
and had his head down in the green stuff. He kept hitting himself with his tail.
THAT shows you how silly dogs are.

BY then I was pretty tired from looking at all these new things, so I lay down for awhile.
"Finally!" my Human said, and went back to the head-rubbing.
I found that pretty boring, and went to sleep.

THE RUSTLING STUFF

SOMETHING must have happened. My Human hasn't been laughing at all lately,
and the long-haired human stopped coming here. (I'm glad about that.)
He's in such a sad state — he makes me lead him around on a string,
just because he saw that dumb dog do it with his human.
HE hasn't a shred of pride. I'd never let anyone lead *me* around on a "leash"
(that's what he calls the string). I really didn't want to do it at first,
but he kept begging and so I decided to let him have his way.
I don't want to make him even sadder than he is.
BESIDES, there are some advantages. I get to go outside now and
discover new things all the time, especially when we walk where there are lots of trees.
Then, too, it's a good feeling to lead a human on a leash.
So I don't mind it at all.

THE other humans we pass look at us and show their teeth.
THEY'RE probably laughing at my Human.
I can't tell for sure.
But if they are, he deserves it.

Sometimes we pass dogs too. Then I climb up onto my Human's shoulders — but only so I can see them better.

When we're all alone, he unhooks his leash from the thing around my neck. I like that, because it shows that he's still capable of being on his own.

When that happens, I play games. I climb a tree and then jump on his shoulder when he's not looking. Or I run away and hide. He just loves stuff like that.

I especially like hiding because these days there are heaps of this rustling stuff to hide under. It's yellow, red, and brown, and it falls out of the trees, too.

I always chase it when I have the chance. Sometimes, all of a sudden, a flock of these rustling things will fly away from the ground. They must be afraid of me, but all I'm doing is trying to play with them. It's hard work though, and I often get out of breath.

Now, only yesterday it was an especially nice day.
There was wonderful warm light,
and we played hide-and-seek among the trees.
Suddenly, a lot of the rustling things tried to fly away from me.
I did my best to catch them all, but there were just too many.
I couldn't decide which one to catch first because they all look so much alike.
I tried running in all directions at once, but that didn't work;
by then I was getting pretty mad.
Then, all of a sudden, they were just lying there without moving at all.
I didn't know which was which anymore.
That surprised me so much that I had to sit down and think about it.

At that moment, something nice happened:
my Human laughed! Really laughed.
"Oh, Jacob," he said, "you look like an idiot!"
(I'm sure "idiot" is something nice, because he was laughing when he said it.)
I was very proud of myself,
and I led him home without making him beg me this time.

AUTUMN FOG

THERE haven't been any of those fuzzy balls around lately. I don't know why. I miss them a lot.
Yesterday I did hear one go "peep! peep!"
But when I ran to the window I couldn't see anything. So I walked over to my Human.
SOMETIMES he makes a funny face to see if I'll be surprised.
Even when I am surprised, though,
I never give him the satisfaction of showing it.
BUT now he was sleeping and I didn't want to wake him.
He's still very sad, so I just let him sleep.
After all, this sadness of his may be contagious.

WHEN I jumped back up to my seat in front of the window I still couldn't see anything —
not even trees or anything.
I couldn't understand it, so I went to the kitchen and had a drink of water.
Then I went back to the window to take another look, but nothing had changed —
still no trees, no *anything*!

LATER that day, my Human went for a walk with me. You still couldn't see much outside, but it wasn't quite as bad as when you looked from *inside*. It was like smoke, but it didn't smell as bad as the smoke that comes from the sticks my Human often holds in his mouth.

ACTUALLY, it didn't have any smell at all — it was just damp. You could see humans and trees, but only sort of. I didn't like it one bit.

Also, I could feel the air pushing against my fur. (It was probably this air that made the funny smoke move around, too.) Wow, it was cold and wet everywhere. And these big drops of water kept falling from the trees and hitting me all over.

I noticed that the rustling things weren't rustling anymore, either — they just stuck to the ground because everything was so wet. In fact, it was so wet that, no matter where I put my paws, they still got soaked.

It was so unpleasant, in fact, that I stopped walking. I decided I just wouldn't lead my Human any farther. I think he felt the same as I did, because he put me on his shoulder and carried me home. It's really nice when we understand each other so well.

As soon as we got home he made himself that hot stuff to drink.
It always makes him silly.
I had to clean myself thoroughly before I did anything else.
For some reason, my Human didn't get silly this time.
He just sat quietly at the table, staring off into space.

I tried to cheer him up by playing with him, but it didn't work.
So I tried all kinds of flying leaps and even tried to catch my tail.
The tail business usually works — but not this time.
I didn't know what else I could do.

FINALLY, I jumped up on the table (even though I'm not supposed to do that) and just stared at him — but very nicely.

AT first he did nothing. Finally he said "Oh, Jacob," blinked his eyes in a peculiar way, and reached out to stroke my back. And he did laugh a little. I was really happy, so I purred up a storm for him.

THE LOOKING BOX

Now it's gotten really miserable outside
and I'm glad I don't have to take my Human for walks anymore.
Sometimes drops of water fall down from somewhere up there, and sometimes white stuff too. But it never stays very long. Then a whole lot of cold air pushes up against the window so that it's not fun sitting there anymore. Still, it's nice and warm inside our apartment, and everything is in its proper place, so that we can feel really comfortable.

I'm glad to say that my Human is normal again. These days different humans come to see him,
and they eat and drink together, and laugh and make a lot of smoke.
They're much too loud for me,
so I go sit on top of a tall chest in the place outside our big room.
I can see everything from there.
Best of all, they can't pet me when I'm up there —
which is what they always want to do when they've had a lot to eat and drink.
I usually don't mind being petted,
but when they eat and drink so much their breath makes me dizzy.

WITH my Human normal again, everything could be really great here.
But now he's gotten a big box
and he just sits in front of it all day when there are no other humans around.

VOICES come out of the box, and I can see humans on the side of the box and other things
that I know about. The strange thing is that all these humans and other things
are much smaller than usual. I know they're not *real* humans,
because I could smell them if they were.
I'VE tried sitting next to my Human and watching the box with him,
but I've never been so bored in my life. So I tried playing instead.

WHAT irritates me is that my Human sits there in front of this thing and just stares at it.
Sometimes his eyes look very strange, too.
THERE are times when he laughs, but not very often.
When that happens I look too, but there's never anything funny going on.
THE worst thing is that my Human ignores me when he's staring at the box.
I can't even get him angry.

LITTLE by little, I've gotten to hate this "looking box," as I call it.
I even tried scratching it once, but that didn't work too well because it's so smooth.
And it didn't even try to defend itself.

FINALLY I got so mad that I did something to annoy both of them. I just jumped up on the table and scattered all the little sticks that my Human uses to make those lines on paper. Then I knocked over a jar (he has a lot of those).

MY Human was so furious that he even forgot about the box. He jumped up and started chasing me around the room. Was that fun! HIS face kept getting redder and redder, and he was saying things that I decided not to understand.

NATURALLY, he couldn't catch me. And when he wanted to stop playing this game, I'd just knock something else over and we'd start up again.

BUT I have to admit that he's smarter than I thought. Now he just laughs when I do knock something over, and he says nice soft things to me.

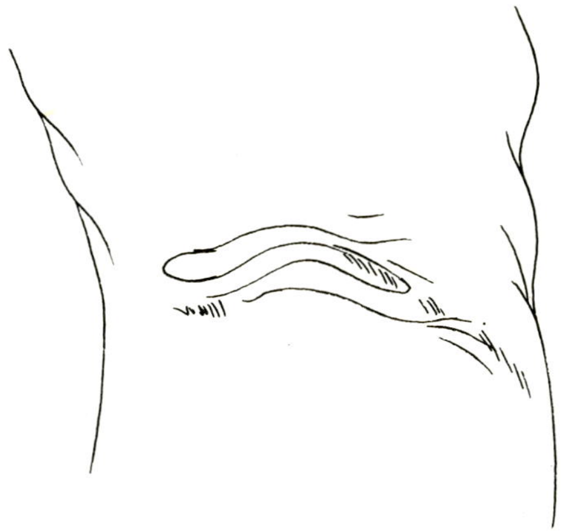

THEN he puts me in his lap and pets me. Only he keeps staring at that box while he does it.
I guess I don't care — as long as he keeps petting me.
AFTER all, I've never seen him try to pet the box!

THE YEAR ENDS,
or THE IMPORTANCE OF BEING PATIENT

Whenever my Human comes home now his paws are very cold and his face is bright red. The white stuff from outside sticks to the hair above his mouth and to that soft, upside-down bowl that he wears on his head. As soon as he gets in the house he shakes himself so that the white stuff flies around. Then he rubs his front paws together and hangs his soft bowl, and his outer fur, on the inside tree we keep next to the door.

Next, he makes himself some hot, black water. It smells good, but tastes awful. When he's especially happy he sings, too, but in such a loud and unpleasant voice — you should hear it! Nevertheless, I'm glad that my Human is feeling so well. When the light outside the window is gone, he makes small fires on the ends of some sticks that we have standing around the room. Then it's nice and cozy here in our apartment.

THERE'S a very nice smell in our apartment now. It comes from these pretty, little colored things that we keep in a bowl on the big table.

MY Human eats a lot of them. Sometimes he gives me one,

but I just sniff at it and lick it once or twice to let him know that I appreciate the thought.

FRANKLY, I'd much rather have a good piece of liver.

But there's no point in expecting my Human to understand this — he doesn't know any better.

The longer I live with him,

the more I learn to be patient with him.

AFTER all, it's not easy being a human.

First U.S. Edition 1981 by
Barron's Educational Series, Inc.
113 Crossways Park Drive
Woodbury, New York 11797

The title of the German edition is:
Jakob—Ich Und Mein Mensch
Kleine Katzengeschichten

International Standard Book No. 0-8120-2391-9

PRINTED IN HONG KONG